HATCHIMALS™

MAGICAL ADVENTURES

STICKER ACTIVITY BOOK

There are lots of smiley Sealarks flipping their tails in this book. How many can you count? Look through the pages, then write your answer here.

welcome to HATCHTOPIA!

The Hatchimals' world is a magical place of harmony and adventure. There are buttercups made of real butter, sunflowers that shine, and bluebells that ring! Get to know the Hatchimals' world and use the clues below to correctly label each location on the map.

PLACE NAME	CLUE
LILAC LAKE	A popular Hatchimal hangout near Fabula Forest.
GIGGLE GROVE	The Giggling Tree is an enormous tree at the heart of Hatchtopia!
GLITTERING GARDEN	This garden grows large sparkly flowers!
CLOUD COVE	Hatchimals love to fly up here—the views are beautiful!
WISHING STAR WATERFALL	This stunning waterfall catches shooting stars.
CRYSTAL CANYON	A canyon made of twinkling gems, nestled in the mountains!
POLAR PARADISE	The chilliest place in Hatchtopia—it's full of ice and snow.
FABULA FOREST	The trees here are pink, green, and purple.

ADD YOUR CUTE HATCHIMAL STICKERS TO COMPLETE THIS SCENE!

3

WHO'S NEXT?

These Hatchimals have come up with an amazing puzzle for you! Look carefully at each row, then choose the right sticker to complete the pattern they've made. Who will it be? A cute Zebrush, maybe, or a smiley Koalabee?

DID YOU KNOW . . .
The speckles on Hatchimal eggs tell you which family they belong to!

FARMYARD FUN

When it's a sunny day, the Hatchimals come out to play! Today Koalabee and his friends are having fun at Friendship Farm and Glittering Garden. Find the missing sticker pieces, then complete the picture.

DID YOU KNOW...
Some Hatchimals from Friendship Farm nest in sunflowers!

HELLO, HATCHLING!

A gorgeous new Hatchling has been born! What kind of Hatchimal has hatched out of the egg this time? The name is hiding in this grid. Can you find it? It's as easy as one, two, three!

1
Cross out all the letters that appear more than once in the grid.

2
Track down the letters that are left.

3
Write the letters in the order they appear to spell the name!

C	I	M	F	H	J	P	G
B	A	C	S	U	C	Y	D
Q	O	V	K	X	Q	R	N
F	H	W	N	T	S	O	J
J	Y	W	D	V	G	C	M
X	Q	M	Z	C	Z	P	G
K	L	A	P	S	F	E	K
F	G	V	C	D	N	I	H

THE HATCHIMAL IS A

_B U T E *_ .

BURTLBE

6

? Stick a picture of the newborn here!

KIDS WILL BE KIDS!

Have you ever raised a Hatchimal until it's all grown up? Congratulations! Your Hatchimal remembers everything that you taught it, but now it's ready for more fun and games! Use this quiz to test your knowledge of the kid stage.

1 What phase of life does the kid stage come after?

a. The baby stage ☐

b. The adult stage ☐

c. The toddler stage ☐

2 What does a Hatchimal sing when it has grown up to a new life stage?

a. "Hatchy Birthday" ☐

b. A nursery rhyme ☐

c. A lullaby ☐

3 A Hatchimal kid will . . .

a. Not know how to walk ☐

b. Know how to walk, but not how to talk ☐

c. Know how to walk and talk ☐

4 If your Hatchimal kid is sick, how can you make it feel better?

a. Rub its tummy ☐

b. Put it to one side ☐

c. Turn it upside down ☐

5 Which one of these is a real Hatchimals™ game?

a. Hatchimal Dominoes ☐

b. Hatchimal Bingo ☐

c. Hatchimal Says ☐

6 When your Hatchimal kid's eyes flash red, what game is it ready to play?

a. Tag ☐

b. Silly sounds ☐

c. Psychic Hatchimal ☐

DID YOU KNOW . . .
Kid Hatchimals love to party, dance, and have fun!

7

MEET AND GREET

New Hatchimal characters are hatching all the time! The lovable critters have glittery wings, wide eyes, and big friendly smiles. Would you like to get to know some of them a little better? Use your stickers to complete these Hatchimal profiles, figuring out which picture belongs with each bio.

NAME: Blue Koalabee

PERSONALITY: Pioneering

NEST TYPE: Warming Willow

FUN FACT: Blue Koalabee loves learning new things about the world around him.

NAME: Blue Elefly

PERSONALITY: Principled

NEST TYPE: Glowing Grass

FUN FACT: Blue Elefly will always stand up for her friends and do what's right!

NAME: Green Hedgyhen

PERSONALITY: Loving

NEST TYPE: Lullaby Grass

FUN FACT: Green Hedgyhen is a sweet Hatchimal who loves to snuggle.

NAME: Orange Tigrette

PERSONALITY:
Daring

NEST TYPE:
Orange Ferns

FUN FACT:
Orange Tigrette likes climbing and flying to all the highest spots in Hatchtopia.

NAME: Polar Draggle

PERSONALITY:
Innovative

NEST TYPE:
Forevergreen Trees

FUN FACT:
Polar Draggle likes to find clever new ways to get things done.

NAME: Purple Puppit

PERSONALITY:
Goofy

NEST TYPE:
Lullaby Grass

FUN FACT:
Puppit is hilarious—he's always making the other Hatchimals laugh!

NAME: Polar Penguala

PERSONALITY:
Fearless

NEST TYPE:
Forevergreen Trees

FUN FACT:
Polar Penguala loves the ice and snow of her Polar Paradise home.

NAME: Pink Bunwee

PERSONALITY:
Playful

NEST TYPE:
Rosebush

FUN FACT:
Pink Bunwee loves to play fun games with all her friends in Hatchtopia!

MYSTERY MAZE

Tigrette is missing her friend Kittycan!
Can you get them back together again?
Put your finger on the start panel, then find
a route through the maze.

TIGRETTE'S GOLDEN RULE:
You can only move forward on the orange squares.

START

FINISH

Stick a picture of Tigrette and Kittycan here!

10

LOOPY LETTERS

Bunwee has something important to say. Can you translate it? Grab a pen or pencil, then write every third letter into the box at the bottom of the page.

Decorate Fabula Forest with more trees and flowers.

Write your answer here.

H O L D ! H A T C H ! P L A Y !

DID YOU KNOW... Hatchimals love hanging out at the Lilac Lake—but if they go for a swim, they come out purple!

11

DOT-TO-DRAGGLE

Draggles are often shy. Sometimes they need to be coaxed out of their shells! Will you help this little Hatchimal say hello to the world? Use a pencil to connect the dots, and then color in the Draggle.

GOOD NEWS! This Draggle belongs to you! What will you call him? Turning the page might help you decide . . .

EGGS-TREME COUNTING!

New Hatchimal eggs are appearing in our world every single day! All they need is your love to help them hatch into adorable Hatchimal babies. How many new arrivals are waiting on this page? Count the eggs, then write the total in the box.

Can you spot the one egg that has started to hatch?

Write your answer here.

22

When you're done counting, add even more magical egg stickers!

THE NAME GAME

What is your favorite Hatchimal name? Whether you've got your own egg already, or you've always wanted one, you've come to the perfect place! Work your way across the page, putting a star sticker beside the words you like best.

1 TITLE

PRINCESS

MISS

MR.

SIR

QUEEN

CAPTAIN

2 FIRST NAME

HATCHY

ROSIE

BARNABY

SNUGGLES

CUTIE-PIE

VIOLETTA

FLUFFY

3 MIDDLE NAME

- ⭐ SNUGGLES
- ⭐ CUTIE-PIE
- ⭐ PINKLE
- ⭐ BUTTONS
- ⭐ SHIMMER-BLINK
- ⭐ MINTY

4 LAST NAME

- ⭐ HATCHERSTON
- ⭐ BOOGIE-WOOGIE
- ⭐ McFLUFFERSTON
- ⭐ SNUGGLEMUFFIN
- ⭐ HATCHEM
- ⭐ EGGHURST

Now put your starry words together and write your Hatchimal's new name here!

DID YOU KNOW... Whenever your Hatchimal reaches a new stage, it will sing "Hatchy Birthday" in celebration!

Answers

PAGE 1

There are four Sealarks inside this book: on pages 5, 6, 10, and 15.

PAGES 2-3
WELCOME TO HATCHTOPIA!

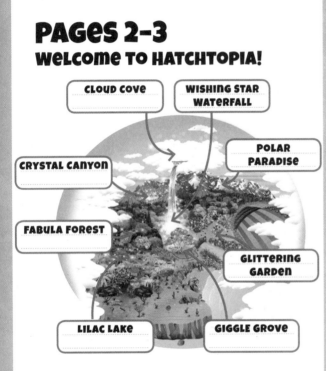

- CLOUD COVE
- WISHING STAR WATERFALL
- CRYSTAL CANYON
- POLAR PARADISE
- FABULA FOREST
- GLITTERING GARDEN
- LILAC LAKE
- GIGGLE GROVE

PAGE 4
WHO'S NEXT?

1.
2.
3.
4.

PAGE 5
FARMYARD FUN

PAGE 6
HELLO, HATCHLING!

C	I	M	F	H	J	P	G
B	A	C	S	U	C	Y	D
Q	O	V	K	X	Q	R	N
F	H	W	N	T	S	O	J
J	Y	W	D	V	G	C	M
X	Q	M	Z	C	Z	P	G
K	L	A	P	S	F	E	K
F	G	V	C	D	N	I	H

The Hatchimal is a BURTLE.

PAGE 7
KIDS WILL BE KIDS!

1. c   4. a
2. a   5. c
3. c   6. a

PAGE 10
MYSTERY MAZE

START

FINISH

PAGE 11
LOOPY LETTERS

HOLD! HATCH! PLAY!

PAGE 13
EGGS-TREME COUNTING!

There are 25 eggs.